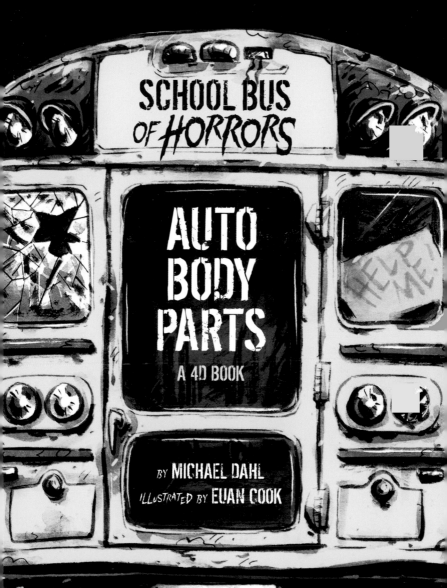

SCHOOL BUS
OF HORRORS

AUTO
BODY
PARTS

A 4D BOOK

BY MICHAEL DAHL
ILLUSTRATED BY EUAN COOK

HELP! ME!

STONE ARCH BOOKS
a capstone imprint

School Bus of Horrors is published by
Stone Arch Books
A Capstone Imprint
1710 Roe Crest Drive
North Mankato, Minnesota 56003
www.mycapstone.com

Cataloging-in-Publication Data is available at the Library of Congress website.
ISBN 978-1-4965-7832-7 (library binding)
ISBN 978-1-4965-8016-0 (paperback)
ISBN 978-1-4965-7837-2 (eBook PDF)

Summary: Aboard a strange-looking bus, a girl hears whining coming from beneath
her seat. When the girl investigates, a hand reaches out and grabs her leg. Then
another hand grabs her and another! Are the body parts reaching for help . . . or do
they want something more?

Designer: Sarah Bennett
Production Specialist: Tori Abraham

Cover background by Shutterstock/oldmonk

Printed in the United States of America.
PA49

1 Ask an adult to download the app.

 Capstone 4D
Education

2 Scan any page with the star.

3 Enjoy your cool stuff!

―――――― OR ――――――

Use this password at capstone4D.com

auto.78327

TABLE OF CONTENTS

From dawn to dusk, the **SCHOOL BUS OF HORRORS** rumbles along city streets and down country roads, searching for another passenger. Yellow, black markings, dirty windows—it looks like any other.

But **BEWARE!** Step aboard this bus and

experience the scariest ride of your life . . .

CHAPTER ONE
HANDS AND ARMS

Iris and her classmates hurry onto a strange school bus. Today is a field trip.

It's easy for the students to find seats. Many students are home sick.

Some have been sick for weeks.

"This bus is so old," Iris says.
"And hot!"

"Big deal," says a boy across the
aisle. "Just crack open a window."

SWISH! BANG! The bus door closes.

The boy across the aisle opens his window.

Then a voice rumbles through the air. "Keep all hands and arms inside the bus."

The teacher smiles. "You heard the bus driver, children," says Mrs. Cogg. "Inside the bus. We all must do our part."

CHAPTER TWO
RING FINGER

Mrs. Cogg walks by Iris's seat and then stops.

"What's that on your finger?" the teacher asks Iris.

"Oh, nothing," says Iris.

The boy across the aisle hangs
his arm out the window.

Mrs. Cogg frowns. "Harvey!
What did the driver just say?"
she asks. "Hands inside the bus."

"But it's so hot in here!" Harvey
complains.

When the teacher turns away,
Iris stares at the large purple ring
on her finger.

The ring belongs to Iris's classmate,
Serena, who always keeps the ring in
her desk.

But Serena is home sick today.

Iris plans to put the ring back
in Serena's desk after the field trip.
Then no one will know she took it.

*It looks better on my hand than on
Serena's,* thinks Iris. *Her hands have
too many freckles.*

CHAPTER THREE
UNDERFOOT

SSKKRAAAAAYYP!

A sound makes Iris look up.
The bus is traveling between walls
of trees.

*Did a branch scrape against the
window?* she wonders.

SSKKRAAAAAYYP!

The sound is coming from below her foot. A crack in the metal floor grows wider.

Iris watches as a small object pokes through the crack.

A finger!

Then another finger.

Finally, a hand reaches out from the crack—a hand covered in freckles!

"Ahh!" Iris screams. But at the same time, the driver hits the brakes.

No one hears her.

Mrs. Cogg rushes to the front of the bus. "Driver, why did you stop?" she asks.

A low voice rumbles. "The engine. The bus needs more parts."

The hand near Iris's foot has slipped back into the crack.

Iris sees the driver getting up
from his seat. He moves like a
shadow out the door.

Mrs. Cogg runs after him.
She wants to know what is wrong.

When she leaves, the students
cheer. They jump from seat to seat.

UUUNNHHHHH! Iris hears a grunt.

The driver is now standing outside her window.

"More parts," he says through the dirty glass.

CHAPTER FOUR
BODY WORK

Iris stares at the bus driver.
She can't speak.

The driver moves like a smudgy
shadow on the glass.

BANG! BANG!

He is working at the side of the bus, just below her window.

The driver said something was wrong with the engine, thinks Iris. *But the engine is at the front of the bus.*

What is he doing?
Iris wonders.

"More parts," comes a voice.
"More parts."

The voice sounds like a young girl.

The freckled hand reaches out and grabs Iris by the foot.

"**AAAHH!**" Iris bends down to free her foot.

KRIKK!

Her ring catches on the edge of the crack.

"My hand is stuck!" cries Iris. "Help!"

The girl's voice drifts up from the metal crack. "Yes," it says. "We can always use a hand."

No one is on the bus to hear Iris scream again.

No one sees her get dragged through the crack in the floor.

CHAPTER FIVE
MORE PARTS

Darkness and heat surround Iris.

She smells gasoline and burned rubber.

She hears a thudding sound. It shakes through her body.

"You!" says a voice.

Iris sees a girl's face in the dark.
"Serena," she cries.

"I suppose you want your ring back," says Iris.

She twists at the purple ring, but it won't come off her finger.

"Who cares about a ring?" says Serena. "This bus will not move without us."

The darkness grows thick. Iris sees more bodies around them.

She recognizes all of the students who are sick and out of school.

"What are you talking about?" asks Iris.

"The bus," says Serena. "The bus needs a hand."

Serana grabs Iris's hand and pulls her toward a lever.

The sick children are standing by other levers. They move them up and down.

"Keep it moving," they chant. "Keep it moving."

The children crowd around the two girls. "Without us, no bus. Without us, no bus."

"We all must do our part," says Serena.

SCREEEEEEEEE-EEEEEEEEEEEE!

Mrs. Cogg climbs back on the bus. The students quiet down.

No one notices that Iris is missing.

One of the students, Lacey, jumps into Iris's old seat.

A dark blur moves from the door to the steering wheel.

The bus starts up again.

WHOMP! KLINK! There is a bang and a rattle.

"Now what on earth is wrong?" asks Mrs. Cogg.

"More parts again," rumbles the voice from the steering wheel.

"We'll need new parts."

Lacey hears a tiny sound below her.

She sees a hand reaching out
from a crack in the floor.

A finger on the hand wears a
large purple ring.

GLOSSARY

AISLE (ILE)—the path that runs between seats on a bus

COMPLAIN (kum-PLAYN)—to show anger, pain, or sadness

GASOLINE (GAS-uh-leen)—a flammable liquid for fueling engines

LEVER (LEV-ur)—a bar or rod used to run or adjust something

RUMBLE (RUM-buhl)—to make or move with a low, heavy rolling sound

SMUDGY (SMUJ-ee)—stained with spots and streaks

DISCUSS

1. Why do you think the author titled this book *Auto Body Parts*?

2. Do you think other students will join Iris beneath the floor of the bus? Why or why not?

3. What is your favorite illustration in this book? Explain why it's your favorite.

WRITE

1. Create a new title for this book. Then write a paragraph on why you chose your new title.

2. In this book, the bus driver is described as a shadowy blur. Write a story about where the bus driver came from.

3. Write about the scariest bus ride you've ever experienced.

AUTHOR

MICHAEL DAHL is the author of the best-selling Library of Doom series, the Dragonblood books, and Michael Dahl's Really Scary Stories. (He wants everyone to know that last title was not his idea.) He was born a few minutes after midnight of April Fool's Day in a thunderstorm, has survived various tornados and hurricanes, as well as an attack from a rampant bunny at night ("It reared up at me!"). He currently lives in a haunted house and once saw a ghost in his high school. He will never ride on a school bus. These stories will explain why.

ILLUSTRATOR

EUAN COOK is an illustrator from London who enjoys drawing pictures for books and watching foxes and jays out his window. He also likes walking around looking at broken brickwork, sooty statues, and the weird drainpipes and stuff you can find behind old run-down buildings.

SCHOOL BUS OF HORRORS

AUTO BODY PARTS

NIGHT SHIFT

OOZE CONTROL

SHOCKS!

CRUSH HOUR

DEAD END

DESTRUCTION ZONE

FRIDAY NIGHT HEADLIGHTS

THE SQUEALS ON THE BUS

UNDER THE HOOD